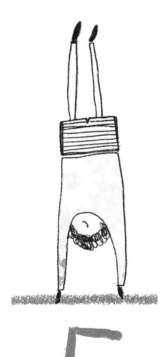

5

6

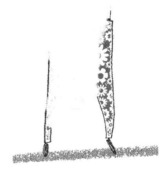

7

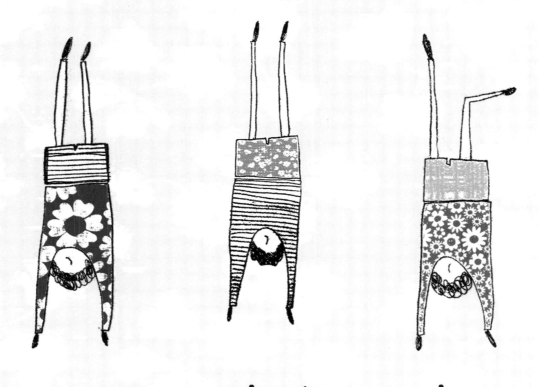

Handstand

dith and Richard

First published in the United Kingdom in 2016 by
Pavilion Children's Books
1 Gower Street
London WC1E 6HD

ISBN: 9781843653127

A CIP catalogue record for this book is available
from the British Library.

10 9 8 7 6 5 4 3 2 1

Printed by Dream Colour, Hong Kong
Reproduction by Mission Productions, Hong Kong

This book can be ordered direct from the publisher at the website
www.pavilionbooks.com, or try your local bookshop.

Handstand

by lisa stickley

My name is Edith. I am little.

I am bigger
than I was last year,
but not as big as I
will be next year.

I like handstanding a lot.

Last Monday I did a handstand and it lasted for 1 second. It was quite a good one but I have only just learnt how to do them. I am still practising.

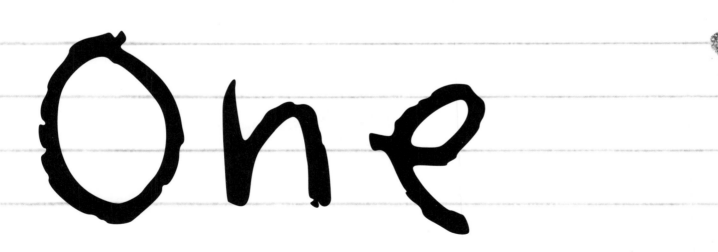

One 1

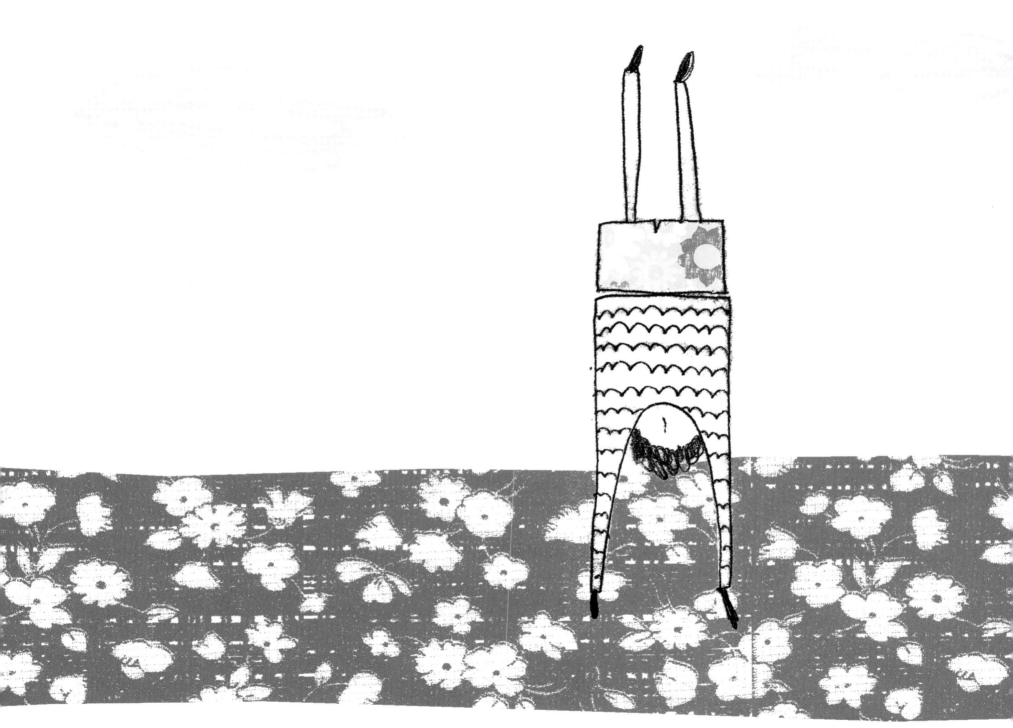

I did a handstand in the garden on Tuesday and stayed up for 2 seconds, until a worm poked his head up out of the grass and made me jump.

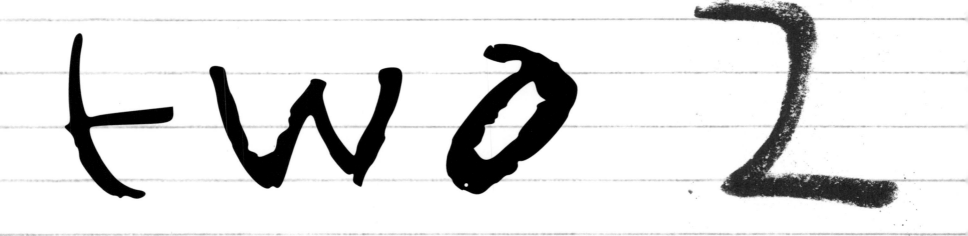

two 2

'Excuse me, did you see that?' said the worm.

'I was on the go, wiggling about and minding my own business when I popped up above ground to find a GIANT hand next to my preferred popping-up place!

'It frightened the wiggle right out of me.'

I practised handstanding on Wednesday in the park. I stayed up for 3 seconds. I fell down because a bee was buzzing around my ear and made me wobble. Silly old bee.

three 3

'Excuse me, did you see that?' said the bee.

'I was busy buzzing along when I went to buzz on that pink-coloured flower, only to discover that it wasn't a flower at all!

It was an ENORMOUS ear!

'Who put that there?'

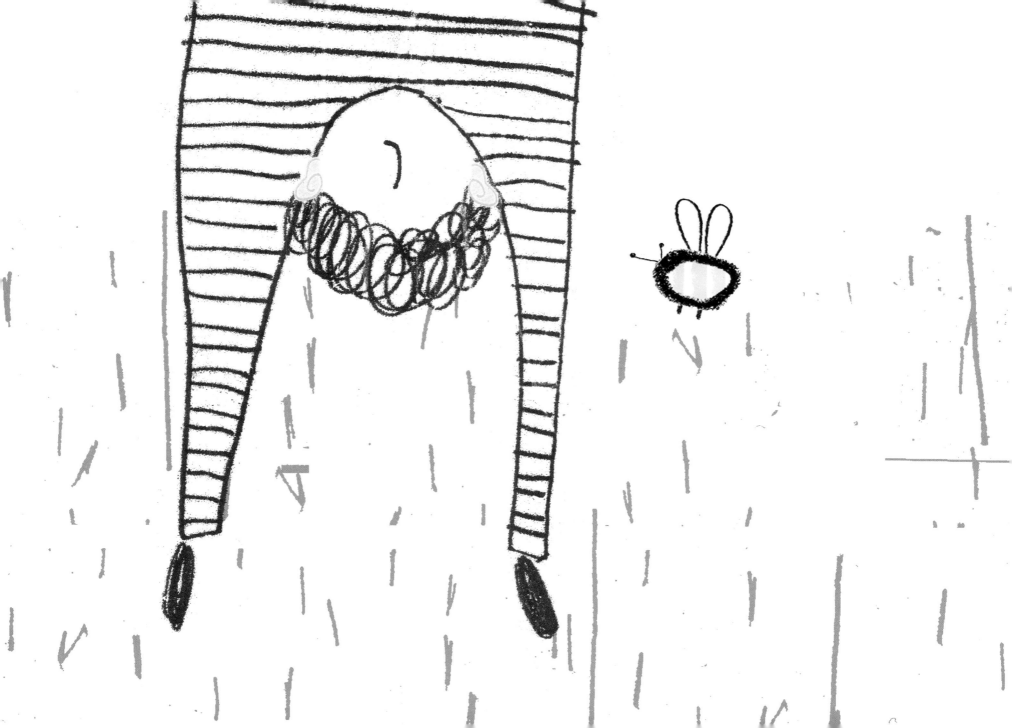

On Thursday I did a handstand that lasted for 4 seconds. It was quite good until a bird did a whoopsie which almost landed on my hand! Yuck!

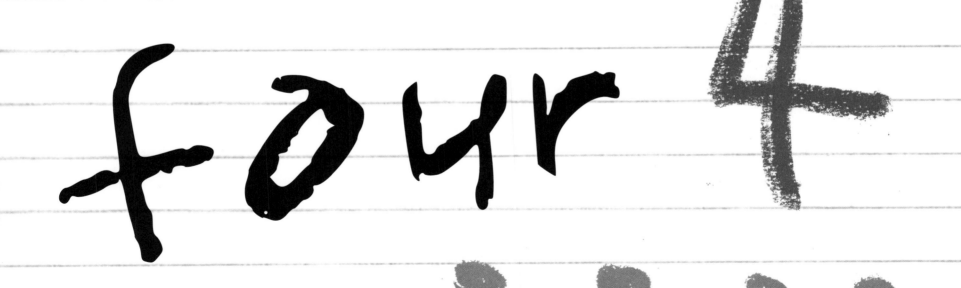

four 4

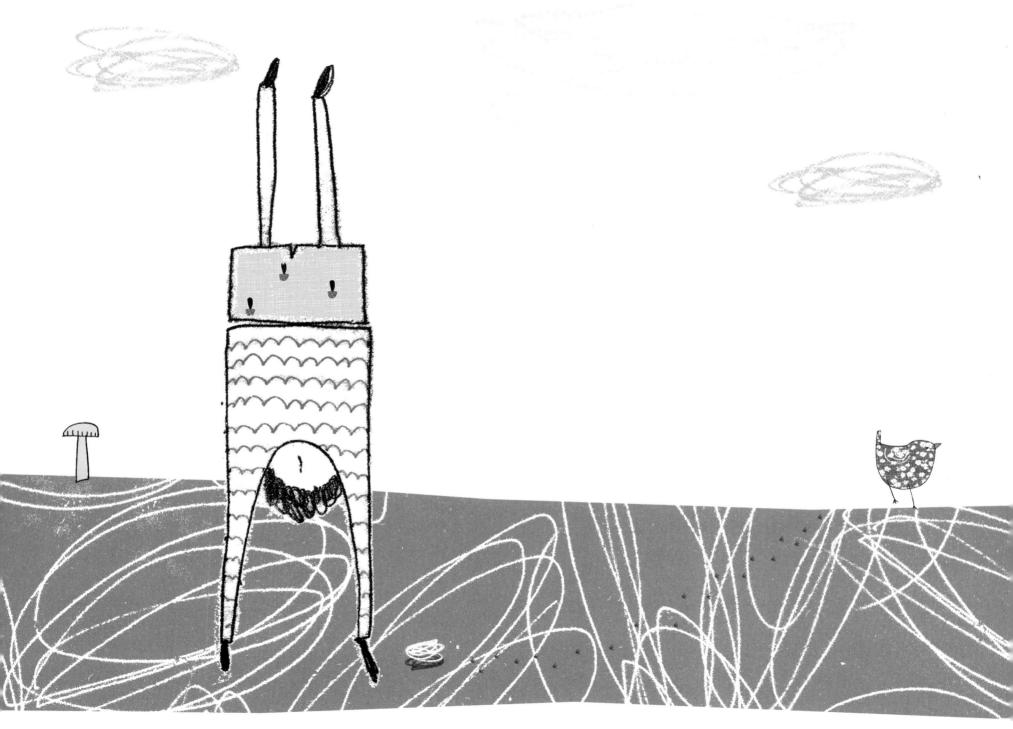

'Excuse me, did you see that?' said the bird.

'There were two big feet swaying in mid-air in my favourite garden so I aimed, and fired, and I almost got a direct hit!

'It was very good target practice. I only missed by a snippet!'

On Friday I did a handstand in the park with mummy. I stayed up for 5 seconds, leaning against a tree. This was much easier until a spider crawled down my leg and it tickled. Otherwise I would have lasted <u>much</u> longer.

five 5

'Excuse me, did you see that?' said the spider.

'I was minding my own business doing my daily descent down the tree when everything suddenly went dark!

'On reflection I think I must have ended up in somebody's shorts.

It was all a bit of a shock really.

Who put them there?'

On Saturday I did a single handstand for 6 seconds. Daddy held my legs. It helped a lot.

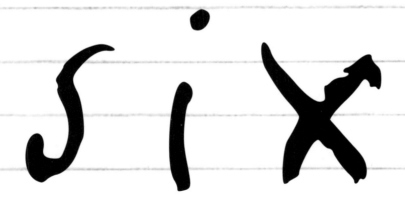

six 6

I don't think daddy can help all the time, holding my legs, as he has weeding and pruning to do.

Also he likes to sit on his deckchair sometimes reading the paper.

I will have to keep practising on my own too.

I did 7 handstands in a row on Sunday. Mummy and daddy clapped. Then we had a lolly.

seven 7

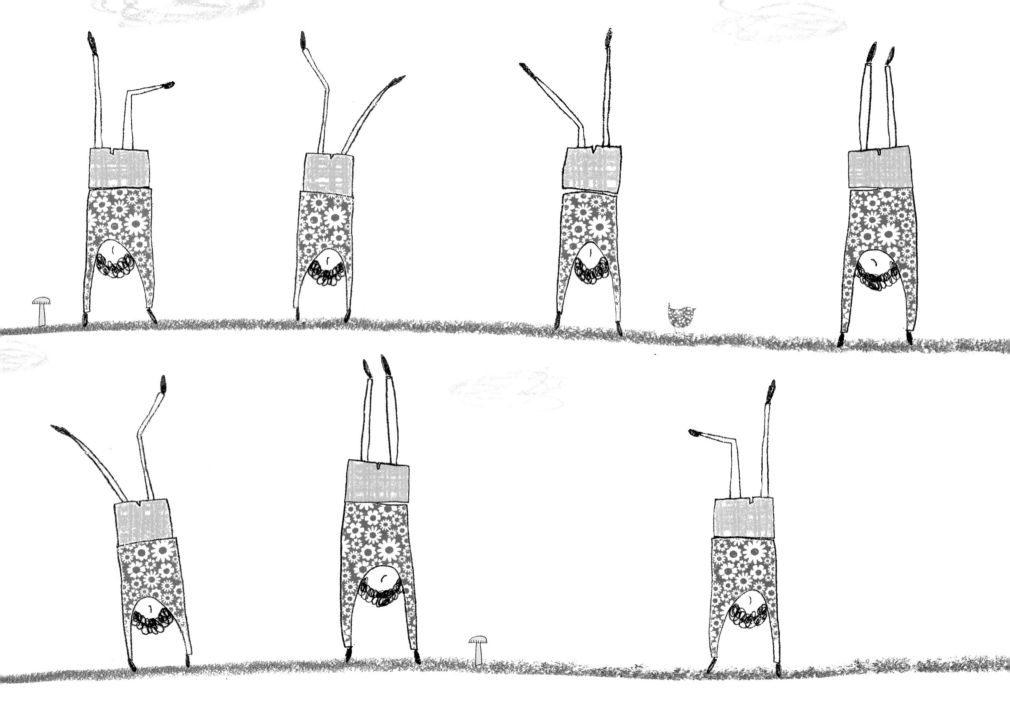

It's quite hard to eat a lolly
whilst handstanding.

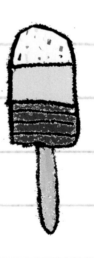

It's much easier when you lean against
the fence!

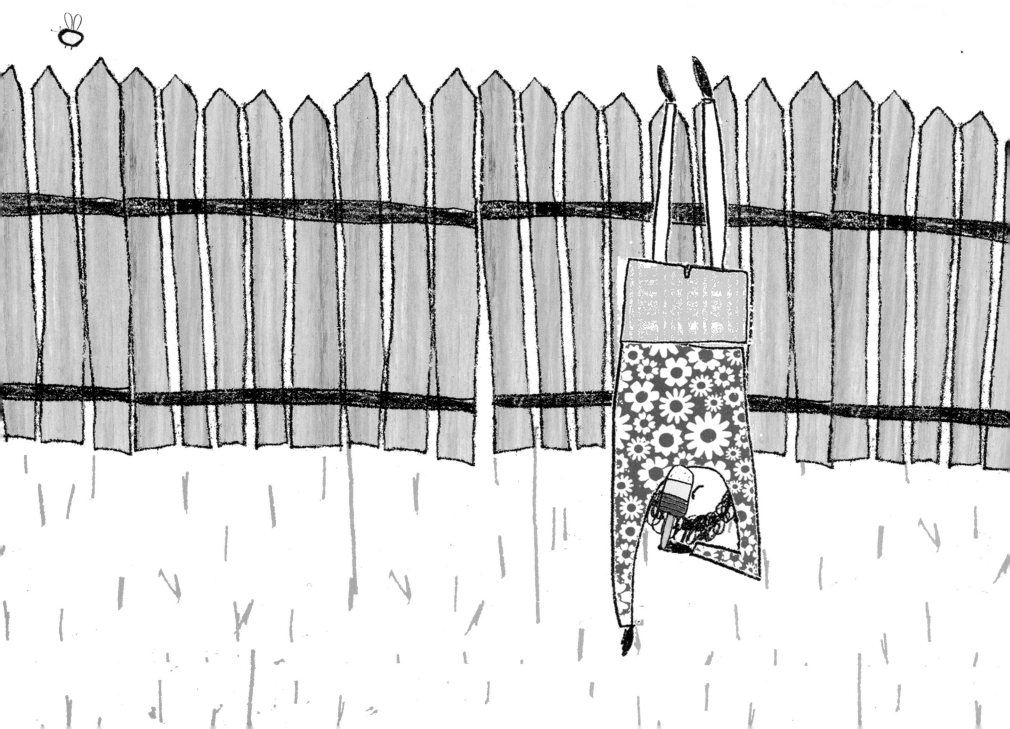

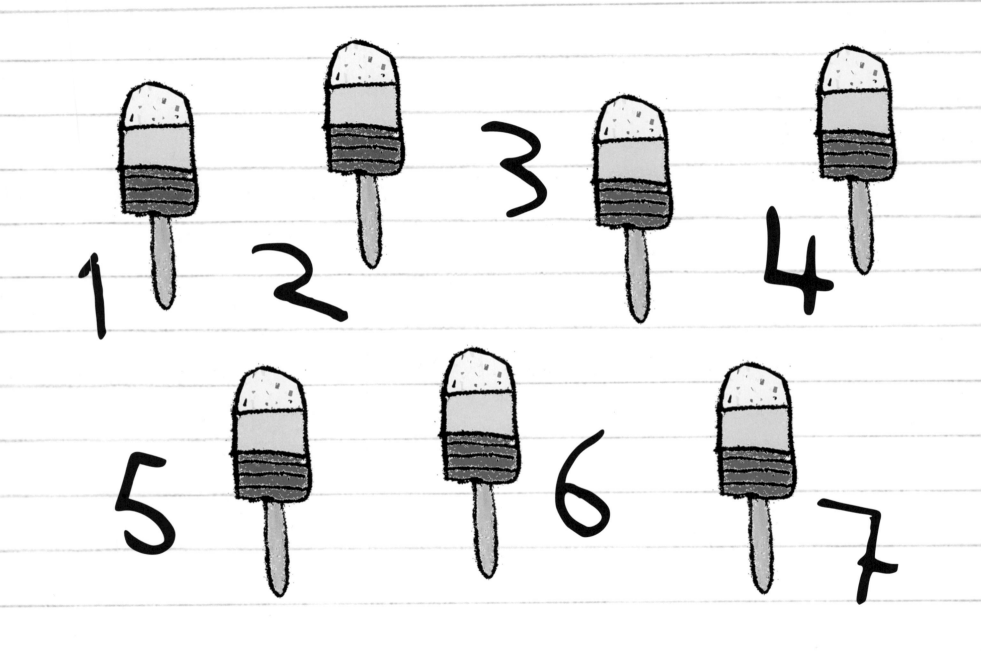

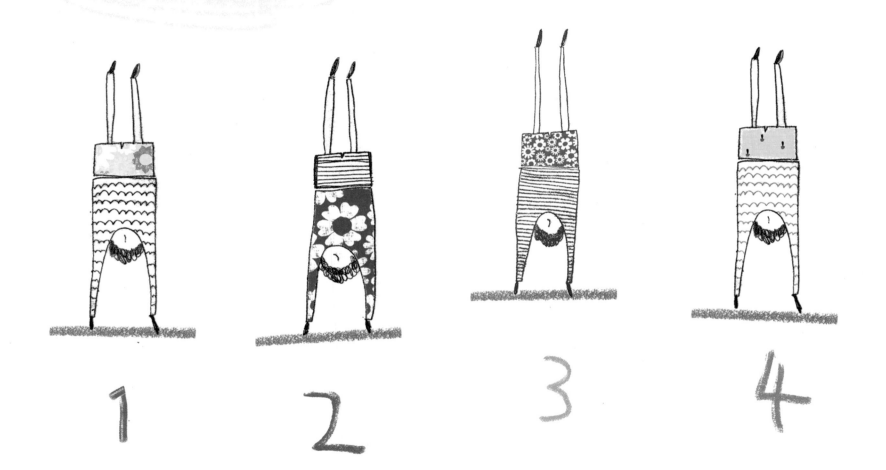

1   2   3   4